W9-BWW-934

3 1389 02635 9265

*For Augie, who is learning how to defend his own turf these days*

ABOUT THIS BOOK

The illustrations for this book were digitally drawn and painted in Adobe Photoshop using a Monoprice tablet. This book was edited by Andrea Spooner and designed by Dave Caplan and Kelly Brennan. The production was supervised by Erika Schwartz, and the production editor was Annie McDonnell. The text was set in Alice, and the display type is Kentucky Fried.

Copyright © 2021 by Elise Parsley • Cover illustration copyright © 2021 by Elise Parsley. Cover design by Dave Caplan and Kelly Brennan. • Cover copyright © 2021 by Hachette Book Group, Inc. • Hachette Book Group supports the right to free expression and the value of copyright. The purpose of copyright is to encourage writers and artists to produce the creative works that enrich our culture. • The scanning, uploading, and distribution of this book without permission is a theft of the author's intellectual property. If you would like permission to use material from the book (other than for review purposes), please contact permissions@hbgusa.com. Thank you for your support of the author's rights. • Little, Brown and Company • Hachette Book Group • 1290 Avenue of the Americas, New York, NY 10104 • Visit us at LBYR.com • First Edition: February 2021 • Little, Brown and Company is a division of Hachette Book Group, Inc. • The Little, Brown name and logo are trademarks of Hachette Book Group, Inc. • The publisher is not responsible for websites (or their content) that are not owned by the publisher. • Library of Congress Cataloging-in-Publication Data • Names: Parsley, Elise, author, illustrator. • Title: How to catch a clover thief / Elise Parsley. • Description: First edition. | New York : Little, Brown and Company, 2021. | Audience: Ages 4-8. | Summary: "When a wild boar with a passion for clover discovers a rare patch in the woods, he is determined to patiently stand guard until it blooms—but he is not the only clover enthusiast in the forest, and it takes reading a good book for him to figure out the mystery"— Provided by publisher. • Identifiers: LCCN 2019033971 | ISBN 9780316534284 (hardcover) • Subjects: CYAC: Clover—Fiction. | Books and reading—Fiction. | Boars—Fiction. | Gophers—Fiction. • Classification: LCC PZ7.P2495 Ho 2021 | DDC [E]—dc23 • LC record available at https://lccn.loc.gov/2019033971 • ISBN: 978-0-316-53428-4 (hardcover) • PRINTED IN CHINA • APS • 10 9 8 7 6 5 4 3 2

# Elise Parsley

# HOW TO CATCH A CLOVER THIEF

L B

LITTLE, BROWN AND COMPANY

NEW YORK    BOSTON

The stems were tall. The leaves were large. Roy couldn't believe his luck—all this clover patch needed were those sweet white blossoms and then he could gobble up his very favorite snack. They were nearly ready. He just needed to be patient.

"Don't even think about stealing
my patch of clover, Jarvis,"
said Roy, eyeing his neighbor.
Jarvis shook his head.

"Heavens, I wouldn't think of it, Roy.
After all, clover is hard to come by
in these woods, and you found it first.
It clearly belongs to you."

"It does," said Roy.
"Now go away.
It's about to bloom."

"Say, you know what you need,
Roy, ol' buddy?
Here.
This cookbook will help you
plan some new recipes
while you wait for those
delightful blossoms!"

THE LUCKY CHEF
HOW TO
COOK WITH
CLOVER

Jarvis hopped off while
Roy kept an eye
on his clover...

and read the first recipe...

and the second recipe.

Chilled Clover Soup

Clover Salad with Shaved Acorns

The third recipe called
for mulberries and
mushrooms.

When Roy returned
from his foraging—

GASP!

—his patch was smaller.

The next day Jarvis skipped into the clearing. "What's the matter, Roy?"

"Go away, Jarvis. My clover is ready to bloom but there's a clover thief around here, so I've got to stand guard day and night!"

"My, my," said Jarvis. "You know what you're going to need, Roy? A proper campsite. Here. This guidebook will give you all the tips and tricks."

Roy resisted.

But finally, he picked up the book and pitched a tent...

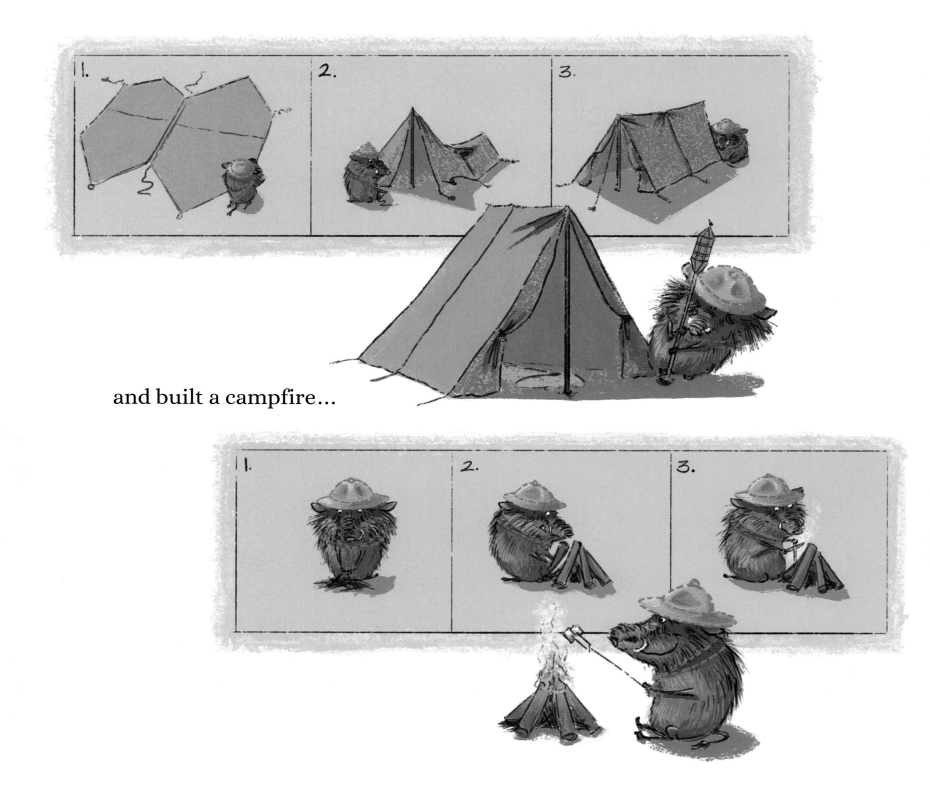

and built a campfire...

and by the time Roy finished
carving out a canoe—

# CRASH!

—his patch
was even
smaller.

NICE

MINE

The next day Jarvis
peeked into the clearing.
"Go away, Jarvis!" Roy yelled.
"I'm hungry and I'm mad and
I've been staying awake guarding
this patch day and night
and that's *all* I will do until
I get my clover blossoms!"

"Roy," said Jarvis,
"do you know what you need?"

"Let me guess…
*another book?*"

"No!"
Jarvis giggled.
"Company!"

"Mind if I—"

# "OH, ALL RIGHT!"

shouted Roy.

"You're going to love this one," said Jarvis. "It's a textbook I've been reading about recent advancements in aerospace engineering."

"I don't even know what aerospace engineering is!" cried Roy.

"You will soon enough! Listen to this."

And Roy listened...
    for a while.

Then it was nothing
but orbital inclination
and nose cones.

When Roy awoke—

# SNORT!

—the clover was completely eaten up,
right down to the nubbins!

"HOW CAN THIS BE?!" cried Roy.

Then he froze and snarled.
"Wait. Where is that gopher?"

"Oh, hi, Roy!" Jarvis gulped.
"Did I hear that your clover
is completely gone?
That's terrible! Sheesh!
And after all you've
done to protect it! So
—*cough*—
what are you going to do?"

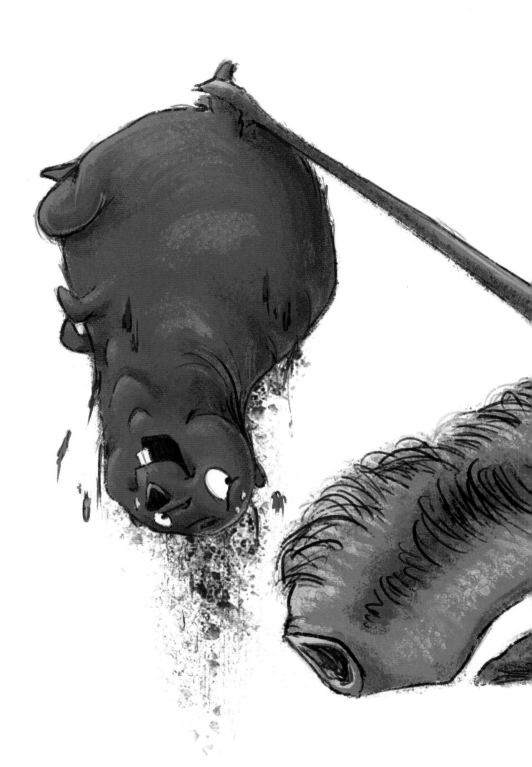

"Jarvis," said Roy,

"I THINK YOU KNOW
EXACTLY
WHAT I'M GOING TO DO."

# "I'M GOING TO GET A BOOK."

Jarvis squeaked.
"Oh, thank goodness!
I mean, of course! A book!
The perfect way to pass the time
while your clover grows back.

Off you go, Roy!"

Roy rushed to the library, and while he waited
for his clover to grow, Roy read.
And read. And reread.
And looked up words he didn't know.
And read some more.

And Roy didn't see Jarvis for weeks.

But when he did…

Roy was ready.

He had just needed
the right book.

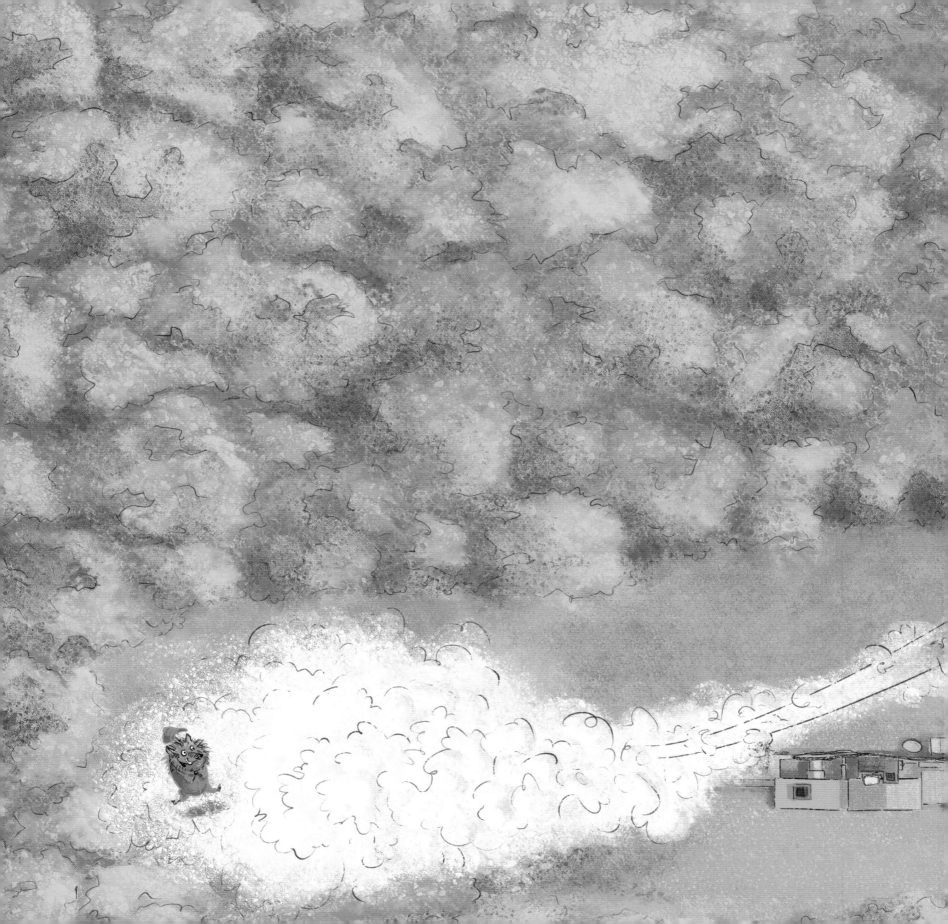